#nofilter

by

Autumn Siders

Printed in the United States of America

First Printing, 2018

ISBN 978-0-578-43147-5

E.M. Sanchez Press
PO Box 472
Wolfeboro Falls, NH 03896

www.butwiththemind.com

For Me;

thanks for letting me be me.

#nofilter

My Mother has no filter,

and she raised me just the same.

All her life she's been a "bitch"

for refusing to play society's game.

I can't imagine a life,

that is forced to fit so neatly in a box.

Living in fear of what might spill over,

knowing damn well that everybody talks.

So, I live my life with no filter,

just the way I was meant to be.

Call me a "bitch" or whatever,

but at least I get to be me.

Haikus

Haikus are more fun

because they take up less space

and yet, still fill holes.

Clowder

Thirty-eight felines,

another neighborhood gang.

Kill you with cuteness.

Gender Bender

Never send a man

to complete a woman's job.

He fights like a girl.

Western Sunrise

Meet me under stars;

stay with me until the sun

rises in the west.

Look Up

Perched upon a branch

a gentle soul watches down;

another looks up.

Music Creates

Music can create

a precious and brilliant light

in the darkest place.

Hi Coo

"Hi," I said to you,

"you wanna' hang out some time?"

"For sure, that'd be coo."

Alarm

Love is 4 a.m.

and you're the perfect alarm

I never will snooze.

Alternative Facts

Freedom is not free,

but you can get a discount;

privilege trumps all.

Genre

Read between the lines,

end up between the covers,

shelve it under "love."

White Coat

Just a light, white coat

but pretty soon you will need

a heavy white coat.

Love

You & I

You
feed my soul,
fill my brain,
tug my heart,
ease my pain.

I
could never
return the favor
but I can
love you
forever.

Summer of '12

It Was the Summer of '69

played on the radio.
However, it was really

the summer of '12.

I could have sworn
you said
that you'd wait forever,
but there was no porch,
no promise,
just a couple months
of pretend.

The summer didn't last
forever,
should've known
we'd never get that far.

But still,
it's fun to remember
what happened
in the back seat
of your car.

Eye of the Beholder

Beauty is in the eye of the beholder.

And 'tis you who holds my eye.

You hold my soul, my breath, my heart, my life.

Carry it all gently and with love,

Protect my being with your warmth.

For trusting another with such precious cargo

Is as challenging as being trusted in return.

Gibroni

I remember the smell of cookies
and the fizz of an opening coke.
I remember you were my shelter
as well as my inside joke.
I remember the pop
as the ball hit my mitt
and I remember the days
when we just shot the shit.
I remember the shuffle
and the doling of cards
and I remember the sun
as we mowed the yard.
Me recuerdo los libros
y los cuentos extraños.
Me recuerdo la risa
y los "feliz cumpleaños!"
Still to this day,
I think fondly of you
and how you changed my world
and made me who I am too.

Dashboard Light

You even look beautiful
by the dashboard light
like under the moon
you lit up last night.
Each mile behind us
and I fall a little more
for your gentle curls
and that cute little snore.
The blacktop ahead
as we race away from dawn
and by the time we are west,
my heart will be gone.

We Met Online

I saw your picture
just one time
and I knew quickly,
that you were mine.
That sparkle
within your eye
and your smile
just makes me cry.
So many miles away
but my heart beats for you
and without a doubt
I know just what to do.
Whoever said that love
can't be found online
has never seen a tail wag
from a creature so divine.

Georgia

Georgia was your name,
at least for one night,
when we watched the sun set
and the moon rise in the sky.
Conversation never dulled
and eyes never tired
as you lay in my arms
talking for hours.
The sun rose slowly,
but faster than we desired,
and back to Georgia you went
dreaming of a life you'd not acquire.

Luto

You still steal my thoughts
from time to time
and I wonder why,
wishing I left you behind.

I guess it's true
that you are a part of me
and I of you.

But, I wish it not
to be so.
I try so hard
to let you go
as the distance between
grows and grows.

I never would wish you ill,
but sometimes I think
of how you are probably
drowning in a drink
and though it shouldn't,
it makes my heart sink.

You had fallen down the stairs
that don't even exist
and had your throat slit
by a cat who was pissed.
You fell and bumped your head
and now you lay dead
as the bugs settle in
making your flesh their bed.
You drown in the tub
as it carried you away,
claw feet scurrying
with no reason to stay.
You were killed by a madman
who got the upper hand
and left your corpse alone
as he fled to another land.
You choked upon a feast
and as you gasped for air
your final thoughts were "really?
I was killed by cat hair?"
You were run down by a car
or you were hanged with a cat toy,
you were eaten by a lion
or you were poisoned with soy.
All of this and more
is what ran through my mind
in thirty-two short minutes
were all the ways you died.

And then you called me back
to reveal behind the shroud
as you said, "sorry I couldn't hear,
the vacuum was too loud."

Extinguished

Your mouth on mine,
no space between,
skin on fire,
burns like gasoline.
Fingers trace,
no spot untouched,
hearts beat fast,
gently clutched.
No words are said,
but still so clear,
unspoken promises,
dreadful fear.
Eyelids flutter
and two souls meet,
the flame extinguished,
but not the heat.

Share the Moon

You forgot our song
just as quickly as you
forgot your promise
and the tune faded
as the words died
on your tongue.
If I sang back the words
would you even know
how much they meant to me
the night we shared the moon?

Summer Grass

That night
as we sat
on the last
of the summer grass
and the moon
and the stars
shone down
on two lost souls;
my arms
wrapped 'round
the only one
who ever got me
and your fingers
laced with those
of the only one
who ever loved you.

On Writing

Aged

Ink stained fingers,
sorrow-drenched heart,
words poured to paper
as salty tears start.

Flame to wax,
wax to paper;
sealed to paper,
emotions caged,
set free one day
by fresh eyes
only slightly aged.

Writer's Block

Sometimes,

when I have writer's block,

I scribble on my page

so it looks

as if I am

writing,

offering some sage

piece of wisdom.

Fake it

'til you make it

has never been
more true.

Blinks

The cursor blinks,
or was it a wink?
An all-knowing presence

who knows a little
too much.

Words fight
for their spot
on the page,

a jumbled mass
on its way
to
the
grave.

A cacophony

of pain
waiting its turn
so impatiently.

So many things
and yet not enough

to exit my brain
still a diamond
in
the
rough.

Synapses fire
like a loaded gun

leaving smoke
and a victim

in their wake.

And still,

a cursor blinks.

The Inner Shelf

Readers can be defined

by what fills their shelves.

They amass a collection

that reveals their true selves.

Writers are harder to peg

as they hide their true self

for the tomes that they create

are on their inner shelf.

Pen to Paper

Pen to paper,

I rush to complete a thought

knowing I am your only savoir

I am master of your plot.

Your life is in my hands

to do with as I please

I can make you live or die

I can be such a tease.

Your story may end here

or continue on in time

the choice is mine to make

and it can turn on a dime.

But, don't think that I don't care,

whatever your future may be

it matters more than you think

because you are a part of me.

Writer's Den

A time and a space,
a peaceful place.
A cup,
a pen,
paper,
and den.

A line and a cause,
a heart full of flaws.
A desk,
a book,
a feeling,
a look.

Format

Words flow or they don't
and characters come to life
with a bit of heart, soul, and ink.

Scribble on a scrap
or type away
but words become the feelings
you mean to say.

This is the easy part,
I've come to find
compared to fitting words
on a page so confined.

Fonts and spacing
don't seem to flow
but they sure can flourish
a little heart and soul.

No H8

If I don't make it home,

there are a few things you should know.

I've hidden money in our spot

in case I had to go.

My favorite memory of life

is the day you stole my heart

which would have been second

to the family we hoped to start.

Please know I didn't want this,

as the choice was not mine to make;

my choice is always you,

it's another's choice to take.

The press will say it's all your fault,

but believe me, it's just not true.

Hatred claimed my life that day,

not my love for you.

January 20, 2017

Magazine

You're like something
out of a magazine;
50's housewife,
model supreme,
hiking maven,
centerfold dream,
scientist chic,
punk and steam,
agile and athletic,
a one-woman team,
movie star gold,
and ready to stream,
you fill every page,
your eye with gleam
each picture revealing
another layer unseen.

Can You Imagine?

Can you imagine
being evicted
by a landlord
who took your land?
Can you imagine
being welcomed
only then to have
that door slammed?
Can you imagine
leaving all you know
for a better life
on a distant shore?
Can you imagine
dreaming so big,
not just rags to riches,
but a little bit more?
Can you imagine
what is only a dream
since the color of your skin
is a little less white?
Can you imagine
a world without color
where people actually
do what is right?

Color Blind

I wonder how it must be

for those who lack the ability

to view the world and see

all the colors of its beauty.

While it might not be so great,

there is one advantage to date.

With no way to differentiate,

it makes it a lot harder to hate.

How Are You?

Waking up this morning,
will it be my last?
I brush my teeth,
eat my breakfast,
and think about the past.

On my way to school
and these faces all around
hide their fear
behind a smile
and they weep without a sound.

No one has the answers
and everyone's to blame
but lives are being taken
like it's all just a game.
Human lives should matter
and prayers will just not do;
if only we took the time
to ask a simple, "how are you?"

Waking up this morning
and I just can't take the pain.
One more punch
and one more word
and now my soul is stained.

On my way to school
and these faces all around,
they don't know

                                        all I hide
                        behind this evil frown.

              No one asks the questions
              and everyone's to blame,
            but life means nothing to me
            and I'll never be the same.
            Human lives should matter
            but I know that's just not true
            since no one took the time
          to ask a simple, "how are you?"

Half Mast

The banner yet waves,
albeit lower than norm,
and a nation yet moves
on in full mourn.
Another day,
another death,
another life
put to rest.
What so proudly
we hailed,
and now so proudly,
we failed.
How many more
must give their lives?
Freedom unearned
from merciless knives.
Children are here
and the next moment gone
soon forgotten
by nation once strong.
Then the next time
happens just like the last
and that nation is fueled,
its soul is aghast.
These are the bombs
bursting in air
but still we sit vacant
while our flag is still there.
A call to action,
not a call to arms

in a nation so broken
and full of new scars.
What will it take?
How many lives can we save?
And make proud again,
this banner that waves.

Justified

We all strive

to be justified.

Center,

left,

right.

Maybe if we tried more often

to be less self-centered

we could be a little more

right.

Proud to Be

Who's proud to be an American
and gets to turn his back
on all these human souls?
What compassion he sorely lacks?

I wonder if some patriot,
from way back in the day,
wonders what he died for
since the people still don't get a say.

Imagine

You were the punk,
the class clown,
the troublemaker
all over town.

They talked down to you
tried to put a figure on your worth,
tried to tell you where you fit
in your place on planet earth.

We had so much in common
and yet, nothing at all
but your spirit drew me in
as I slowly broke your wall.

You were the chump,
the jerk,
the kid who never
turned in his work.

They never saw more
than their simple minds could see
and while they looked down on you
they always praised me.

But I knew deep down inside
that there was something more
as you got up on the stage that day
and your singing rocked me to the core.

You were the musician,
the hero,
the messenger to those
who were always zero.

You sat at the piano
and placed your hands on the keys
your green hair combed neatly
as you expelled notes to please.

"Imagine there's no heaven
It's easy if you try
No hell below us
Above us only sky..."

You were Lennon,
you were love,
the brick wall that would not break
no matter how hard they shove.

That was the first time
that I had ever heard that song
and each time I hear it now,
to you my memories belong.

We never spoke more
than a few words here and there
and I am sure to you I was nobody
in my imaginary pair.

But I was awed,
astounded,
amazed at how
your voice sounded.

I think about you sometimes
and what you went on to do
and how you moved me that day
which I am sure you never knew.

I'd like to imagine that the world
stopped trying to hold you down
and that you can live your life in peace
and still be the class clown.

You were the punk,
who sat behind me
in high school Latin I.

Faith

Your faith is astounding
but you lack one thing:
compassion.
Did you forget
you're a human being?

Mismatched Socks

I once knew a girl
who wore mismatched socks,
never combed her hair,
and collected rocks.
She always had a smile
as others put her down
and never showed fear
when others were around.
The more I got to know her,
the more my smile grew
since any gloom was banished
as her laughter cut right through.
She marched to her own drum,
sometimes literally,
and she never quite knew
how much she meant to me.

Poesía

El ritmo

El ritmo de mi corazón

mantiene el tiempo con cada movimiento

y yo sé sin duda

mi corazón es tuyo.

The Rhythm

The rhythm of my heart

keeps time with each move

and I know without a doubt

my heart is yours.

Historia

La historia de mi amor

comenzó con una especie de dolor

que cambió el camino de mi vida

y terminó con una sombría despedida.

Story

The story of my love

began with a kind of pain

that changed my path in life

and ended with a somber goodbye.

La mente pequeña

La boca abierta

los oídos cerrados

siempre resultan en

la mente pequeña.

Small Mind

And open mouth

and closed ears

always ends up

with a small mind.

El mundo real

El mundo real está pintado en la sangre de la angustia,
mezclado con las lágrimas más tristes,
esperando la felicidad para agregar
un toque de color en nuestros corazones.

The Real World

The real world is painted in the blood of anguish,
mixed with the saddest tears,
waiting for happiness to add
a touch of color in our hearts.

Cinco de Mayo

Una victoria poco probable

un ejército tan pequeño

una nación orgullosa

un país con un sueño.

–

Una victoria olvidada

un ejército caído

otra nación borracha

con la sangre de historia.

Cinco de Mayo

An unlikely victory,

an army so small,

a proud nation,

a country with a dream.

A forgotten victory,

a fallen army,

another drunk country

with the blood of history.

Muerte

Las sombras bailan
detrás de mis ojos
y las llamas parpadean
con los dedos rojos.

La noche cae
como una manta caliente
y mis ojos se cierran
permanentemente.

Death

Shadows dance
behind my eyes
and flames flicker
with red fingers.

The night falls
like a warm blanket
and my eyes close
permanently.

Nature

Battle of the Trees

I call it the battle of the trees;
some fell and some still stand,
neither side claiming victories.

Someone else who roams the same
might come across this tragic scene
but they might call it by a different name.

Still, they stand all crissed and crossed,
their fates still to be decided,
neither side knowing who has lost.

Canvas

She crafted a canvas
so perfect
with not a single
drop out of place.
A blue so pure,
no blemishes
I'm sure.
Miles and miles
I can see
what can only be
Dear Mother
at her finest.

T-Storm

The sky darkens
as clouds roll in
and the heat simmers
while the light grows dim.
Winds start to whip
but still the heat won't break
and every living soul
has had all it can take.
The first drop falls fast
and hits like a shot,
splattering its guts,
making a liquid dot.
In that moment it seems
the heat just won't end
until the next drop hits,
a cool, welcome friend.
Finally the sky
opens up with a crash
and rains pour down
as tree limbs thrash.
The first bolt of lighting
is fleeting and weak
but the thunder soon crashes
as the storm reaches peak.
The rain soaks each traveler
straight to the bone
and the winds won't cease
as the old buildings moan.

Just as soon as it began,
each drop takes its leave
and all that remains
drips quickly from the eave.
The summer sun pierces
through the very last cloud
but off in the distance
rolls the thunder, still loud.
The heat may have broken
but just for a while;
so I'll enjoy the moment
with a post-storm smile.

We Are Wrong

White powder
falling from the sky
a facade of cold,
no more than a lie.

Somewhere in the distance
flames burn so free,
mapping destruction
in the wake of trees.

Nature never asked
for this dreadful ruin,
at the hand of men,
ruthless tycoons.

What more will be left
of this scorched earth?
What will become
of Mother Nature's birth?

When is it too late
to repair what is gone?
When do we realize
it is we who are wrong?

Reading Leaves

No one ever talks
about reading dead leaves,
yet they have so much to say,
an obituary of summer
on a crisp autumn day.

Some life
this leaf has lived
under the sky,
still so high,
it's seen all
until it died.

On the ground
crunched by us all
never to rise
from its terrible fall.

Ocean in the Sky

Tonight, the ocean took to the sky.
Waves crashing down on the stars behind.
And the moon flits from tree to tree
lighting the gaps for a second,
maybe three.

The leaves blow up and crunch below.
The trees sway, branches in tow.
The night is young and the ocean wide
and she has the sky's depth
in which to hide.

Emilita

In 2012, a fantastic feline by the name of

Emilita Isabella María Santina Anna Pinta Guadalupe Dominga
Rodríguez Sanchez Scroogè Siders de las Botas

found her way into my life.

I'd like to say that Emilita was fascinated by the words I would write and share with the world, but I think it was more so that she knew she could do better. With these sentiments behind her, she started writing (with a little help from those with thumbs) and sharing her words with the world. The poems and short story (*Front Porch*) that follow are works of art accomplished between naps by *the* cat, Emilita.

My Love

It's not that I don't like you,
I just love myself too much.
The thought of loving another
gets my fur all in a bunch.
I'll love you when there's time
and when it's best for me
just to keep you hanging
on thoughts of what may be.
Don't be offended
by what is simply true;
my love for me is greater
than my love for you.

Riches

Sometimes I think I was wrong
to choose a family lacking riches.
How's a cat to live properly
with access to so few fishes?
But then there are times
when I know I chose just right
like when it is oh so cold
and I cuddle with my girl all night.
But still I think it would be better
to find someone with wealth
since they could afford some heat
which is better for my health.
But then I hear that bag shake
and I am right where I should be,
waiting for my fish to eat
with my chosen family.

Skunked

I just want to be on my porch
and enjoy the summer night
as I wait for my foxy friend,
visible only by moonlight.

I never asked you to come
and I don't get why you are here
this food is not for you,
I thought that I made that clear.

We are both black and white,
that's obvious to tell
but you can be certain we differ
since you quite clearly smell.

So be on your way quickly
and please leave me be
while I wait for my true friend
to join me for tea.

Take it from a Cat

The world is simple from my eyes,
I wish humans could see the same.
A nice nap and a meal will do
or maybe a cat and mouse game.

I fill my days with love for myself
so call me selfish if you will,
but I'll never really hate you
unless you try to give me a pill.

Sure I am not loyal like a dog
but I think my pride's enough
at least I spread no hatred
over superficial stuff.

Yes, I know I've killed,
but just a mouse or two
and not because of hatred
or who they prayed to.

I may not be the best judge
but at least I can see
that love will get me dinner faster
than will negativity.

Lamb

I don't understand
why you won't let me in.
There are battles to fight
and wars to win.
If I could only enter,
I would make you see
that nothing can stand
between that mouse and me.
You think you may know
about who I am
but really I'm not
some cute little lamb.
Ferocious and wild,
I'll attack if I must
'cause I always get my mouse,
in that you can trust.

Sixpence

Why would you ever bake
blackbirds in a pie
when plucked right from nature
is still a taste for which to die?

Four and twenty seems too much,
at least for one cat to try.
These humans have it wrong,
would you believe how much they lie?

And then to think these birds
could strut about and fly?
It sounds a recipe for disaster
that takes off to the sky.

The lesson to be learned
is never to trust the guy
who takes all his recipes
straight from a nursery rhyme.

Plastic Teeth

Your torturous weapon
made of plastic teeth
will haunt my dreams
with constant grief.
For my own good,
this you always say,
but that comb is the devil
in every single way.

Stranger

There's a stranger in my yard
and I am not a fan.
There's a burglar on the loose,
who will catch this man?
There's a woman out there too
and they surely have a plan.
There are strangers in the yard
so it's about time I ran.

Spit and Shine

Your hands better be clean
if you're going to pet the queen.
Do you know how long it took
to achieve this perfect look?
An hour on each paw
is standard feline law
and no one quite knows
how much time is spent on toes.
This shiny coat you see
is natural beauty
but a little spit and shine
is a work that is all mine.

Parkour

They run and jump
and dive and leap
and climb and fly
from tree to tree.
Their bushy tails tall
and their little claws discreet
as they chase each other
with cheetah-like speed.
They flip and flop
and bend and reach
and wrangle up
the kids they teach.

They move about
before my eyes
as I sit and wait.
There is no doubt
I'd eat these guys
if ever my dinner's late.

Rent

I have found a new place to live
and the rent is really cheap
I bargained down to three fish
after all, four seems kinda steep.

This place is perfect you see,
it's got windows and screens
to watch all the squirrels
play in the grass that's so green.

I can't wait to move in
and for when the rent is due,
what were you confused?
You pay me. I'm not paying you.

Cat Calls

"You're so beautiful,"

I know

"You're so wonderful,"

I know.

"What a beautiful tail,"

I know.

"How cute you are,"

I know.

Can't you praise me

and find a treat

at the same time?

Thrill of the Kill

A mouse on the run

is a joy indeed

knowing that the kill

it the only thrill I need.

Just to catch a glimpse,

I would wait for days

in this same spot

just waiting to graze.

You might think I am asleep

and my eyes may be closed

but still I'll catch my prey;

I only need to use my nose.

Hairball

My stomach is turning
and my mouth is so dry;
this hairball inside me
makes me want to cry.
But real cats don't cry
so look how brave I'll be;
I'll roam around until
I find the perfect spot to free
this chunk of hair,
all slimy and gross
and full of saliva
and disgusting to most.
Walking sure helps
but laying even more
so the best spot to be
is on your bed and not the floor.

Best That You'll See

When will you get it?
I do what I want.
So no matter your wishes
I'll go on this jaunt.

I'll sleep in this bed
and I'll eat on this shelf.
I'll do as I please;
it's good for my health.

Your commands are pointless
and your wishes for not.
Your demands are futile
and your hopes, distraught.

But look on the bright side
at least you've got me
and I know for a fact
I'm the best you'll ever see.

Fur-Dried

I know something is wrong,

I can tell from the tears

that seep into my fur,

that much is clear.

I know someone is missing,

though not where he's gone

and I know that I miss him

but tomorrow's a new dawn.

I know why the tears are shed

and I'll allow them for now.

My fur can dry your tears

while I cry out, *meow*.

Front Porch

It was a hot day in July when I witnessed the murder. I was laid up on my front porch that day on account of being a cat. With nothing else to do, I decided to keep an eye on the neighborhood. I was just dozing off when I saw a flash of orange across the street. It turned out to be the bully cat, Scat, who lived in the loud house across the street. He always tried to catch the birds from my yard. Often times, my servants were forced to chase him away making noises loud enough to raise the dead.

Today, however, he was on the run from his captors, Zed and Caliban. Those two were always sure to be bad news. They smoked like chimneys and if I didn't know better, I'd say they were growing something illegal like catnip. I kept my eye open in case Scat tried anything funny. When I was sure he was on his way to the pond, I finally settled back in for a nap.

~

I was just starting to see mice on the back of my eyelids when suddenly,

Clang, Bang, Bounce!

The school boys down the hill were always tinkering with something. If there weren't things to fix, then their favorite pastime was basketball. I craned my neck to get a glimpse of their action. One boy was playing basketball, but the other two were out of sight. Then there was a silence like I had never heard before in this neighborhood. I waited to hear hammering or a car racing up the hill.

Swoosh!

A flock of every kind of bird flew out of the trees across the street. Like straight out of *The Birds*, I feared for my life (that movie was not what I thought it would be). Each winged creature sang a different song, but each just as terrifying as the next. They flew with all their might as I checked my blanket to make sure I hadn't emptied my bladder.

Clang, Band, Bounce!

The boys were at it again.

~

My servant finally arrived to give me a well needed massage and I told her about all the crazy things happening in the neighborhood.

"Nothing good will come from spying," she warned. Boy, was she right. She made me some tuna and then left me to my own devices.

I knew I should be resting since I wouldn't be able to nap for at least another hour, but I couldn't pull myself away from the action. The pesky squirrel was back on the tree. He was an addict. He discovered the hummingbird feeder this spring and it was downhill from there. Whenever he came around, he rubbed his little paws together as he sat jonesin' for a fix. The other critters veered away from him fearing he would go nuts at any moment.

I kindly told him we didn't have what he was looking for, but he insisted on sticking around in hope that we might put a new feeder out for him. Every chipmunk, dove, and woodpecker promptly turned around when they saw the guy. I was ready to go out there myself and take care of the problem when suddenly,

CAW! CAW!

The squirrel ran and the sky darkened above as if night had fallen. Where the poor addict had been just seconds before was a scene I could barely believe.

A murder had landed before my very eyes. Savage and brutal, the black mass filled the yard. A cacophony of screams and caws made my blood run cold. I called to my servants,

"More seed out front!" The gang cawed in agreement and with the hope that they would be hungry nevermore.

I finally settled back in for a long-needed rest, but I knew I would never forget this hot July day when I saw a murder from my front porch.

On the Rocks

A copy of Hemingway's *The Old Man and the Sea* was cracked open on the desk. The hardbound copy was aged from the salty air, just like Harvey. He sat sipping his morning coffee and smoking a cigarette, the only things that seemed to warm his bones on this brisk fall morning. The soothing sound of the waves crashing on the rocks made him feel like he wasn't as alone as he truly was.

It had been three months since Harv had talked to another human. At first he thought he had found heaven, but he missed the company now. He and Sam always had such good conversations. He seemed like such a good guy at first, but the solitude must have driven him crazy. Or maybe Harv drove him mad?

He shrugged the thought away as he thought about the more important things he had to do today. A storm was on its way and his supplies were running low. A chopper was supposed to arrive tomorrow, but most likely the winds would make delivery impossible. Sure, there was more food since he had a supply for two, but he smoked more than enough to make up for the lack of a colleague... *a colleague.*

Was that all Sam was to him?

The two had survived on this rock for over a year together. They were both too old to go to 'Nam and too young to go to their graves, so why not take a job where they could disappear? Just like society wanted them to.

Now, Sam really had disappeared. Harv knew that was a foolish explanation given where they were, but he had no other logic to combat the theory. One minute he was there, the next he was gone. He knew he should have called it in to the mainland, but deep down he kept thinking that one day Sam would just show up and they could go back to how things were.

Harv picked up his cigarettes and threw on his coat. He hadn't set foot in the keeper's quarters above the boathouse since Sam's disappearance. With the storm coming though, he had to board up a broken window. As he walked across the rocks he could feel the salty breeze on his face. He had always liked the sound of the ocean. It always seemed to be whispering secrets just out of his reach. Today the sound calmed him as he focused his attention to crossing the slick rocks.

"*Harvey,*" a voice rang clear amidst the crashing of waves. He stopped dead in his tracks and saw Sam standing twenty yards ahead. He took a step forward and his foot slid out from underneath him. He fell quickly but still tried to break his fall with his hands. Unfortunately, his forehead ended up taking the brunt of it. He staggered to his feet and looked back where Sam had been. There was no one there.

"Sam!?" he called out to the ocean. He looked back down at the rock now stained with his blood. If he was seeing things before he hit his head, what would he see now?

He made it across the rocks without any more damage and stood a safe distance away from the boathouse. Just staring into the vacant house gave him the creeps. He would go upstairs, fix the window and get back to the lighthouse. Climbing the creaky stairs gave him a sense of familiarity the combined with the dread of a terrible nightmare. When he got to the top, the place looked disheveled. Papers were strewn across the floor and the stench of rotted food wafted through the air. Across the room the damp curtains blew around in a violent frenzy. Shards of red glass occupied the floor beneath the broken window. One large piece still remained in the frame, this one a lighter shade of pink.

Harvey took a deep breath and crossed the battlefield into the kitchen. The stench in there was more overpowering as the fresh air hadn't helped that room. He grabbed a toolbox from the cabinet and then removed the door. It was slightly bigger than the window and seemed strong enough to withstand the winds that were on their way.

The last screw from the hinge hit the ground, its metallic trail bouncing out of the kitchen. Harv set the door down on the counter and followed after it. Instead of picking it up, he stared at the window that was already covered. He looked back in the kitchen to where he had set the cabinet door, but it was no longer there. He stumbled backwards into the doorframe. He saw the toolbox was still there, its handle covered in blood. He panicked, and then remembered about his fall on the rocks. It was his blood on the toolbox. He needed to tend to his wound.

With his back to the wall, he inched towards the bathroom. As soon as he made it in, he slammed the door behind him. He reached for the matches to light the lamp on the counter. After a few strikes, the match burst to life but before he could bring the flame to the lamp, he saw the dried crimson that coated the counter and sink. He dropped the match as it burned his fingers and he was out of there before the flame extinguished.

Heavy raindrops fell all around him. The storm was getting closer. The rain helped wash away most of his own blood and he quickly determined that his wound had stopped bleeding. There was a reason he hadn't been in there since Sam left. Sam was gone.

His head throbbed, but there was no way he was going back and he couldn't stay outside much longer. Back to the lighthouse was his only option at this point. Back across the same rocks where he had seen Sam.

The wind was really picking up, but he managed to light a cigarette as he crawled back over the jagged land. His lungs burned with each puff, but it warmed him inside. The waves were crashing down just feet away from him and one wrong step would drag him out to the ocean. That is if he survived the rocks all around him. He just had to make it back to the lighthouse and survive until the helicopter made it tomorrow. He would tell them about Sam and now that he was injured, they wouldn't leave him out there alone. He would get off this rock and never come back.

By the time he reached the lighthouse, he was soaking wet. He climbed the stairs and threw off his jacket. The wet mass pounded the floor as Harv reached for a dry blanket. Wrapping it around his shoulders, he reached in his front pocket for a smoke.

"Shit!" The entire pack was drenched. He went for his secret stash in the desk and noticed his book was closed. A shiver ran through him, but not because of the damp cold. He picked up the book and flipped through it. A photo fell to the floor. Fingers shaking, he picked up the faded picture. The print on the back read, *Sam & Harvey 1969 Midway Lighthouse.* He flipped it over and immediately jumped back, hitting the desk. It was the picture they had taken when they arrived at the lighthouse, but Harvey's face had been scratched out and the grin on Sam's face seemed bigger than he remembered.

With the book still in his hand, he ran downstairs almost losing his footing. He burst out of the lighthouse and the wind blew him back. He pushed forward as the rain pounded against him and he realized he had nowhere to go.

"WHAT DO YOU WANT, SAM? WHERE ARE YOU? SAM?" Harv screamed at the top of his lungs but the roar of the ocean and the wind made it hard to even hear his own voice. His head throbbed and he closed his eyes crouching down between the rocks. On the back of his eyelids, his memories flashed.

Sam was in standing in front of him. They were arguing.

"I love you," Sam protested. The words burned into Harv's mind. "You don't feel it too?" Sam took a step towards Harv.

"Get away!" Harv shoved him and watched as he fell backwards. He heard the glass shatter.

The waves were pummeling against him. He could barely keep his balance nestled between the ocean and the shore.

"help.." Sam's voice was weak and blood poured out of his chest. Harvey looked at him. There was nothing he could do. He picked up his feet and a scream filled the humid, sticky air. He tipped him backwards until he fell out the window. Crunch. Blood stained the rocks below.

"No!" Harv screamed, "That is not what happened! Sam!"

He dragged the body to the boathouse and went back upstairs to board up the window. There was blood everywhere. He tried to wash it off his hands as the sink became a red pool.

He could see something stuck between the rocks in front of him.

"Sam!" he slid closer using this hands and feet to climb down.

He didn't know what to do with the body. It was hot and he wouldn't last long in the boathouse. He went back down to move him. Sam was gone. Sam disappeared.

"I killed you. I killed you, Sam." The words left Harvey's mouth so quietly that the ocean soaked them in before they could go anywhere. He grabbed the lump he had been moving towards and stumbled forward hitting his head again. He fell into the water next to the mass and as he was pulled under he looked into Sam's lifeless eyes. Then everything faded to black as he the ocean pulled a blanket over him.

Mark was not happy about having to bring supplies out to Midway, but at least the storm had subsided. He set the chopper down and helped Steve unload the cargo.

"Sam? Harvey?" There was no sign of life on the remote rock.

They took the supplies to the keeper's quarters and immediately knew something was wrong when they saw the war zone in front of them.

"Stay here, Steve, I will go check the lighthouse." Mark set off across the jagged shore and as he got close to the lighthouse he heard something tapping against one of the rocks. He saw a skeleton moving back and forth with the water, the skull colliding with the rocks and keeping time with the ocean. Mark doubled over and grabbed his stomach. He managed to keep his breakfast down and kept moving to the lighthouse.

Mark ran up the stairs and almost tripped over the coat on the floor. There was no one up there, but on the desk there was a soggy pack of cigarettes next to an open hardbound copy of Hemingway's *The Old Man and the Sea.*

Near-Life Experience

The rain felt like bullets against his skin as Jake raced down the freeway. He had somewhere to be though and nothing would slow him down. He could feel the tires of his '86 Ducati F1A sliding on the pavement below and did his best to keep the bike steady. He tried to keep his mind on the road, but he couldn't help but think of her.

Lucy's laugh was always so contagious. No matter what the problem was, a short encounter with Lucy would help anyone. They first met in third grade. Jake had just moved to Chicago and on his first day of school, she was the only one who made him feel welcome. Since that day, they had been the best of friends and would be until death did them part.

Red lights flashed suddenly in front of Jake and he had nowhere to go. He clutched the brake and held his breath as he waited for the bike to slide. When he let his breath go, he realized his bike had come to a stop and he was still upright and safe on the side of the road. He took a moment to dry off his helmet and resumed breathing normally again. He had near-death experiences before, but each time something like that happened, it brought him closer to life rather than death.

"I dare you to get in this dog cage and roll down the hill." Jake was 12 when Adam made that dare. Adam was Lucy's twin brother and since the beginning of that summer, the three had been inseparable. They stood at the top of the hill in Dan Ryan Woods. They found the rusty dog cage off the running trail and like the dumb and bored kids they were, they decided the best option to kill time would be this.

"Okay, but you have to do it after me," Jake replied. He then climbed into the cage and Lucy latched the door. She and Adam gave the cage a push and it started off slowly down the hill. Jake rolled into the sides of the cage but pretty soon he couldn't tell up from down. Just as he was getting nauseous, he came down hard on his side and pain coursed through his body. His face smashed against the rusted door and he tasted blood.

When the cage finally came to a stop, he heard Adam and Lucy shouting his name. The last thing he remembered before he blacked out was looking into those beautiful blue eyes that belonged to the person who opened the door and rescued him.

He calmed his nerves on the side of the freeway and dropped the bike into first as he set off to one of the hardest things he would ever attend in his life. Jake hadn't been back to Chicago in five years, but he still knew the way as if he had driven it every day. The closer he got to his exit, the rain seemed to slow down.

While he had stayed in touch with Lucy, he hadn't spoken to Adam since he left Chicago. Even when Adam called him a week ago to tell him about Lucy, the conversation was short and emotional. He didn't know how it would be to look him in the eye after how they left things. Lucy had been hurt the most it seemed, but then she didn't understand it all. Now, she never would.

It was the summer before they left for college when Lucy told Jake to meet her and Adam at their spot by the hill. When Jake got there, the sun was just setting and Adam was nowhere in sight. It became quite clear that Lucy had every intention of being alone with Jake. To Lucy, it became quite clear that Jake had no intention of being alone with her.

"Is there someone else?" She asked as tears welled in her eyes.

"No," he responded sympathetically, "it's just that we are going to college and it would be silly to start something now." And that was the first and only lie he would ever tell Lucy. He would never get to tell the truth.

The rain let up as Jake pulled on to that familiar street. As he pulled into the driveway, he cut the engine and didn't take his eyes off the house as he put down his kickstand. He got off the bike and walked up the stairs. As he reached up to knock on the door, he saw the note,

MEET ME AT OUR SPOT

Jake set his helmet on the porch and walked down S. Damen Ave. like he had so many times before. As he reached the hill, the sun was setting. He expected Lucy to be there as he relived a painful moment, but this time it was Adam. His back was turned, but he spoke softly,

"I promised my sister, I was going to start living my life. I told her the truth before she died. She gave me her blessing. This time, I won't take 'no' for an answer from you." Jake felt his heart in his throat. He was unsure of what to say. Adam turned around and Jake looked into those beautiful blue eyes. This time, Jake knew he wouldn't give "no" as an answer.

Pitch Black

Link

"Guys, we are so late! How will we find a table near the tv for all of us?" Dani would be the reason the group was late and she was also the first to complain.

"Girl, it's your fault. Hurry up! You better pray there is a booth for us." Sam didn't really care, he just loved giving Dani a hard time.

"Oh, Satan, our stepfather who art in Hell. We pray you provide us with a booth big enough to accommodate our group of six and close enough to view the game. Amen." I too couldn't resist giving anyone a hard time.

"Amen," chimed in Franny, Sam, and Liz. Jael kept quiet as usual and Dani glared at me with a face that would put Satan to shame.

"Very funny, Link. Let's go. James Taylor is singing the anthem and there is no way I am missing the first pitch!" Dani took her baseball as seriously as she took her fashion. I never understood why she put on all that makeup when she had such a pretty face. Then again, there was a lot about women I didn't understand.

With all of us ready, we walked down D Street to the pub. It was a good thing that Dani lived close otherwise we would never make it before the game started. The crowd would be the most interesting part to me. New England fans were very protective of their Sox. I didn't care but would root for L.A. just to play Devil's advocate. Sam, being a transplant from Tinseltown, would be rooting for them as well. The ladies of Elm Street, Dani, Franny, and Liz were true New England sports fans. And Jael, well she never really showed an interest.

It was one the first cold nights in October which was a rarity being this late in the month. It wasn't just a little chill either, but a cold that dug into your bones. The others raced as if chasing their breath in an attempt to find warmth at the bar faster. I hung back with Jael. I knew she grew up in a religious household and I thought I might have offended her with my earlier comments on Satan.

"I hope you know I was just messing around with those Satan comments."

"You shouldn't joke around about the Devil, you know?" She stopped walking and looked right at me. Or maybe, right into my soul. Just as it got heavy to hold her stare, she started laughing and smacked me on the arm. "You should have seen the look on your face." Chuckling, she jogged off to catch up with the group. I stood there a second longer watching her go. A smile crept across my face and I took a deep breath of crisp, cool air.

Sam

Two years in New England and the cold still got to me. I rushed to open the door for the ladies but really, it was to feel the warm blast of air from the bar.

"Hurry up, Link!" I wasn't about to freeze my ass off for this slow-poke. He jogged up the stairs and I followed him closing the door behind us.

I expected the usual roaring patrons and bottles clinking but was surprised to see the place was mostly empty. More importantly, the large booth with a television was wide open and waiting for us.

"I guess everyone else has cable," Link joked.

"I don't really care. We got a table and I won't miss any of the action!" Dani already had her coat off and was positioned right in front of the television.

"And I won't miss my Mookie!" I didn't know if Franny actually knew how baseball worked or if she just cheered when her favorite player did something.

"I hear when he's up to bat, all bets are off." Link drew laughter from all the girls. I wondered if it was his good looks and charisma or if they actually thought he was funny. One thing I knew was that I fell prey to him too. I couldn't help but smile.

Our waitress came over and to no surprise, everyone ordered a beer.

"I'll have a vodka martini, dirty." The waitress didn't miss a beat, but my crew gave me dirty looks. "What? You can take the boy outta' Hollywood, but you can't take the Hollywood outta' the boy."

"Well the Sox are gonna' knock the L.A. outta' you tonight." Liz pointed to her shirt as she boasted.

"Yeah, yeah. We'll see."

"Ssshhh!" Dani ended our banter. "James Taylor is singing."

The waitress brought our drinks just as the crowd started clapping for James. I took a sip and made a mental note to ask for top shelf vodka next time.

Chris Sale threw out the first pitch of the game to Dozier for a ball. I'd always had a touch of psychic ability. I didn't talk to dead people or anything like that, but sometimes I would get a feeling. In that moment, I knew it was going to be a rough night. The Sox were going to win and I had this absolutely dreadful feeling about it. I didn't know I cared that much about baseball.

The only other time I had a feeling like this was the night before my grandmother died. I had a dream that night and she visited me. She didn't say anything. She came into my room, sat on my bed, and stared at me. It felt so real, but it had to be a dream because the next morning we got a call from the nursing home where she lived and they informed us she had passed early that morning.

"Hello? Earth to Sam." Franny's voice broke into my thoughts. "You just zoned out there. What's in that martini?" I looked down and realized I drank the whole thing. I didn't remember doing that. I had no time to wonder though as Franny, Liz and Dani started to cheer. I looked up at the television just in time to see Mookie Betts cross home. Sox led by one and somehow, I daydreamed through half an inning.

Franny

I can't stand her. She's so weird. Why do we let her hang out with us?

I had all these thoughts every time Jael joined us. She ordered a beer but still hadn't touched it. Meanwhile, Sam had downed his whole martini. It must have been good. My own beer was warm, but I expected nothing less. This place always had the worst service, but it was the closest to our apartment and since we didn't have cable, it was the go-to place for games and booze. Especially on the cold winter nights. It made sense for us to come here. Sam lived in the neighborhood too, but Link and Jael both lived out of town. They worked together at the factory and he invited her along one time last year. After that, she never stopped joining us.

She rarely talked but she sure did listen. She was probably a serial killer. I looked away from the game and there she was just starring at Sam. *She's so creepy.*

Then I looked at Sam and he was creepy too. He was completely zoned out like he wasn't even on this planet.

"Hello? Earth to Sam." He shook his head and looked down at his drink. "You just zoned out there. What's in that martini?" I looked back to the tv just in time to see my main man cross the plate. After some proper cheering for the boys, I looked back at Sam who was pretty pale for a black man. "I think you better switch to water. You look like you've seen a ghost."

"Yeah, I may have. Be right back." He bumped the table as he got up and made his way to the restroom.

"What's his problem?" Dani didn't take her eyes off the tv as she asked.

"I think he downed that martini a little too fast."

"Or, he couldn't stand to see his team losing so fast," Liz offered.

"One run doesn't mean we'll lose. Go Blue!" Link uttered the evil words loudly enough to garner some nasty looks from the handful of people at the bar.

"Ssshhh, you'll get us kicked out of here." Jael batted his arm as she feigned worry. I hated to say it, but I agreed with the weirdo.

"Why don't you go check on him, Link?" I had to send him away before the rest of the bar pegged us as Dodgers fans.

"Why me?"

"Um...'cause none of us can go in the men's room. Someone will have a fit that we are in the wrong bathroom."

"Fine, but someone better cheer for L.A. Jael, it's up to you." She broke her silence with a giggle. Her eyes followed Link as he got up and headed after Sam.

"And then there were four." Liz made spooky sounds right before she cheered for Benintendi crossing home.

Jael looked sour but said nothing. She waited until I turned my interest back to the screen but from the corner of my eye, I saw her switch her full glass with Link's empty glass.

So Weird.

Liz

I didn't know why everyone else bothered coming. It was like they all had better things to do than watch the game. I guess being born and raised in Boston gave me a closer connection to the Red Sox. Watching them play always reminded me of the good times. Daddy was still around. Mom didn't drink. If we couldn't make it to Fenway, we always made sure we were home to watch it on the tube or listen to the games on the radio. Sometimes, when the Sox won, I would imagine my dad cheering like a little kid. I used to think that the only thing he loved more than the Sox was me. He may have loved them more. Or maybe he didn't love anything.

"More beer. Yum!" Link took a sip after he sat back down at the table.

"Is Sam okay," Franny asked.

"Yeah, I think so." Link seemed nervous and quickly followed with, "he didn't feel well though so he said he was just going to go home. Well he will be sad he missed that! Kemp knocked that one outta' there!" Link's excitement drew the attention of the grumbling fans at the bar.

"We're still winning." I had complete confidence in the boys.

The others chatted while I watched a groundout, a walk, and Sale strike out Barnes for the third out. Time for a bathroom break.

"Alright, ladies and Link, someone has to move so I can use the restroom." Franny slid out of the booth so I could go. "Be right back. Don't let them bat without me!"

"Hey, do you want another beer," Dani asked.

"Sure, order me one," I shouted back as I rounded the corner.

The bathrooms were by the back door that led to the deck where everyone went to smoke. I saw the red-hot glow of a cigarette which seemed brighter against the black backdrop of night. I started to push the door to the bathroom when I had a feeling. I headed towards the door to the deck and pushed that open, forgetting all about my planned trip to the restroom. There was a man who looked familiar. I couldn't really see him in the dark, so I guess he felt familiar to me. I took one step out into the cold air and realized who he was.

"Dad?"

"Well at least Liz won't be mad that she missed that uneventful inning. What's taking her so long anyway?"

"Yeah, her warm beer is getting warmer by the second," Franny said.

"Maybe one of you ladies should check on her. Boys aren't allowed, you know."

"I'll go. I've got to use the facilities anyway." Link got up to let Jael out of the booth.

"Alright, Link, what's the deal with her?" Franny wasted no time in starting this interrogation.

"With who?" Link looked puzzled.

"Whom," I corrected.

"You know who. Jael."

"Jael? What's wrong with her?" Link was clearly offended.

"Exactly!" Franny's enthusiasm only ticked Link off more.

"Hey! There's nothing wrong with her. She's just a little different."

"Okay, that's putting it mildly. Still, why does she keep coming out with us?"

"'Cause I invited her."

"Oh!" Realization dawned on Franny. "You like her!"

"What!? No. I mean I do, but not like you are implying."

"I think you should know then, she traded glasses with you when you went to check on Sam. She probably roofied you. How are you feeling?"

"Franny, she didn't roofie me. She took a sip of it and said it was too warm to drink. I'll drink anything, so she said I could have it. I am not going to pass up a free beer. I didn't know you had such a problem with her." Jael came back around the corner and Link stood.

"Liz wasn't in the bathroom," Jael informed us. Instead of letting her back in the booth, Link grabbed their coats.

"I'm not feeling well either. That warm beer must be getting to all of us. Jael, you wanna' take off?" She seemed confused but took her coat as Link handed it to her.

"Sure, Link." He threw $20 on the table.

"Enjoy the game, girls." The bitterness in his voice was quite apparent. He and Jael walked to the door and out into the chilly night.

"Was I rude," Franny asked looking bewildered. I didn't answer but looked back at the tv.

"When did the Dodgers score another run?"

Sam

That was stupid. I can't believe I kissed him.

"God, it's cold." My breath blew back in my face as I uttered the words to no one. My phone buzzed in the pocket of my jeans.

What if it's him?

I pulled my hand from the warmth of my coat pocket and grabbed the phone from my jeans. I looked at the screen. It wasn't a text, just a notification.

Machado singles to left, Turner scores, Freese to second.

Baseball. When this night started, the only thing I wanted was for the Dodgers to win. Simple. Things were not so simple now.

I retreated from my thoughts and looked around only to realize that I didn't know where I was. I was walking on the railroad tracks but for how long, I didn't know. At least there hadn't been any trains or I would have been flattened like a penny. I quickly got off the tracks before that thought became a reality.

I tried to get my bearings, but I soon discovered that I couldn't see any lights from the city. There was no way I could have walked that far, but no matter which direction I looked in, it was pitch black. I spun around again and this time I saw a bright red glow in the distance. I flipped on the flashlight on my phone and started towards it.

As I got closer, I could make out the shape of two people but with each step, the body on the left started to lose its shape. The red glow dimmed out as well. I was within arm's length of the shadows but now there was only one and my flashlight revealed it to be Liz.

Liz

"Hiya, Lizzy." His gravelly voice sounded just like I remembered.

"I knew it. Mom always said you died. That you killed yourself, but I knew that wasn't true. I knew you were alive. Why did you leave?" I felt like this whole moment was a dream and I had so many questions for him.

"It's complicated, Slugger. I didn't want to go, but I had to. I made a deal. It was when I was young. And stupid. It came back to bite me in the ass. I'm sorry." Those two words held more emotion than I had ever heard from my dad.

He took another drag from his cigarette and the glow lit his face up enough to tell that it was him, but something was different. I just couldn't tell what. He wasn't how I remembered him.

"Are you back?" My voice sounded just like the littler girl I was when he left instead of the woman I had become.

"No. I'm sorry." I'd never heard or seen my dad cry, but his voice trembled and I thought he was going to. "Let's walk, Slugger."

I realized that my coat was back at the table inside when the frigid air bit straight to my bones. I still couldn't make out Daddy's face even though the street lights should have shed light on it. He remained in shadow no matter how I looked at him.

"Why are you here if you can't stay?"

"I'm here on business."

"Where have you been?"

"Where it's warmer." I laughed. At this point in time, that could be anywhere. "I've missed your laugh."

"So why don't you stay? I miss you."

"It's not up to me. I'm sorry."

"Stop saying sorry!" All the years of his absence boiled over with those two words. "You don't get to come back and say sorry and expect it to be all better. You left! You were everything to me and you just walked away so easily." The explosion of my feelings warmed me a little but the chills came back as he puffed on his cigarette again and this time I saw his eyes. They were black. Hollow. Emotionless. This *thing* was not my father.

"It wasn't easy. I'm so sorry, Lizzy." Those were his last words as he threw his cigarette to the ground, stomped on it, and left me again.

Link

Sam kissed me. I liked it. I'm not gay. Why did I like it? Why did I like Sam? I should be freaking out right now, but I liked it.

"You're awfully quiet over there." I must have been walking too fast because Jael was out of breath trying to keep up with me.

"Sorry, just upset."

"Yeah, I can tell. If it's because your friends don't like me, don't worry about it."

"It's not that they don't like you. They just have trouble understanding people who aren't like them."

"So, they don't understand anyone?" A shy smile crept across her lips and I couldn't help but smile too letting out a chuckle in the process.

"I think you are right. But that doesn't make it right for them to treat you this way."

"No." We walked in silence before she added, "but don't you believe in karma?"

"I've never seen it, so I guess not."

"There is plenty that you can't see, but it's still there." We stopped in front of her car and her eyes looked up into mine.

"Look, Jael…"

"I know. It's okay. I think you and Sam would make a cute couple."

"What? How did you…"

"Oh come on, you'd have to be blind not to see that you two like each other."

"I didn't even know I liked him until half an hour ago!"

"You must be blind. Fear not, 'love looks not with the eyes but with the mind.'"

"Are you reciting poetry to me?"

"From the Bard himself." She giggled like a schoolgirl.

"You're a complex girl, Jael."

"All girls are complex, Link. See you tomorrow."

I waited until she got in the car and locked the doors before I started off down the street to my own car. I pulled my phone out and saw that I had three missed calls from Sam. He was probably freaking out that he overstepped boundaries or upset me. There was only one voicemail so I hit play. Sam's voice was filled with terror.

"Link, please help. I'm...somewhere. On the railroad tracks. Liz is here. We don't know what is going on. It's so dark. Please. The railroad tracks... *Clank!*"

What was happening? Was he that upset that he was trying to kill himself? No, Liz was there.

I stopped wondering, put the phone back in my pocket, and ran back towards the railroad tracks near the bar.

Franny

"Going into the sixth and the boys are winning five to three! I can't believe Liz left."

"Her coat is still here, Franny, and her wallet." Dani stated all of this with no concern.

"If I hadn't been to check for myself, I wouldn't believe Jael that Liz was gone."

"Can we not talk about Jael?"

"What, you're still blaming me for everyone leaving? At least this way we can watch the game in peace."

"Don't you think it's weird that she left without her coat in 30° weather?"

"Not if she met a cute boy to keep her warm." I laughed, but Dani did not join me.

"I don't know, Franny. Maybe we should try to look for her." Concern finally flashed across her face.

"Okay, you wanting to miss baseball? This is serious. I already texted her like twenty times. She hasn't responded to any of them. Do you think we should call the cops?"

"No," Dani responded quickly. "Let's see if we can find her. Why waste the taxpayers' money if she did in fact meet a cute boy and ran away with him?"

I called the waitress over and we settled the tab. Dani grabbed Liz's coat and her own and we trudged out into the icebox.

Tonight was so not playing out the way I planned it. Apparently I was public enemy number one, Liz was missing, and now I was missing the end of the game and freezing my ass off at the same time.

"Where do we even start?" I felt overwhelmed.

"Maybe we just check and see if she went home?"

"Right. Hey, is that Link running at us?" Part of me hoped it was him and not some deranged madman, but the other part knew he could be a deranged madman when it came to his sentiments towards me at the moment. He was breathing so hard that it looked like he was smoking. He slowed down when he realized it was us.

"Where are you going, Speedy?" Dani didn't seem taken aback that he had just been charging at us seconds ago.

"Sam..." words formed between gasps for air. "Tracks...trouble...Liz too."

"Woah," I stopped him from talking any more. "Liz? She is with Sam?"

"Why is she with Sam," asked Dani.

"I don't know." His breathing started to get back to normal. "Sam called me and said he and Liz were on the railroad tracks but he sounded weird."

"Where's Jael," Dani asked.

"She went home. Look, I'd love to stay and chat, but I have to find him."

"We'll come with you." Dani offered our services without my permission.

"Lead the way, Link." I motioned for him to carry on and we headed down the railroad tracks.

Sam

"Call him again!" Liz was having a nervous breakdown. I don't know how I wasn't joining her. Maybe because I was so cold. I'd given her my jacket when I discovered that you can in fact hear a person's teeth chatter when she's cold enough.

"Okay, but this is probably the last time. My battery is just about done for." I knew he probably wouldn't answer but I still felt like he was the only person to call. The phone rang and rang and I heard his baritone voice,

"Hey you missed me. Drop a line and I'll get back 'atcha."

"Link, please help. I'm...somewhere. On the railroad tracks. Liz is here. We don't know what is going on. It's so dark. Please. The railroad tracks..."

Clank!

I dropped the phone,

"Shit!"

"You broke it! What was that?" Liz's franticness escalated severely.

"I don't know but now we can't see shit. Shit!" Liz tapped the screen of her watch but the dim light did nothing to pierce the darkness and illuminate what caused the noise. "Alright, let's stay calm. Someone will find us. We just have to stay here. The worst thing to do is move when someone is looking for you.

"Is someone looking for us, Sam?" I didn't know what to say, so I opted for nothing. "I'm scared."

"I know, Liz. Me too."

Dani

The tracks were dark and our cellphones made it just bright enough so we wouldn't trip. Link was in a hurry, Franny couldn't keep up, and I was somewhere in between the two.

"There was some sound on the voicemail," Link started to explain. "Like metal on metal or something. It was odd.

"The whole thing sounds odd. Are you sure this isn't some sort of payback for the Jael thing," Franny asked between attempts to catch her breath.

"Go back if you want, Fran, but Sam's in trouble." Link couldn't be bothered by anyone who tried to slow him down right now.

"I hope everyone's batteries are charged," I said.

"I know, it's still five to three but going into the bottom of the sixth. Maybe the boys will extend their lead!"

"I meant for our flashlights, dummy."

"Oh. Yeah. I suppose that's good too."

"Ssshh," Link stopped ahead of us signaling us to do the same. "Do you hear that?"

Clank...Clank...Clank...Clank...

"Sam! Liz!" Link's voice broke through the silence and must have startled Franny since I saw her jump.

"Link! Over here!" Sam's voice called back from the dark. Link took off in the direction of his voice. I followed with Franny still bringing up the rear.

"Sam!" Link shouted again, still unable to find him.

"Link!" Sam's voice was clearer this time and Link's flashlight hit on two bodies up ahead. He stumbled as he ran across the tracks towards them. Sam was already making his way to Link and caught him before he could fall.

"Together again," I proclaimed. This night was turning out just the way I wanted.

Liz

I was cold. Colder than I'd ever been in my life. I wanted to move just to stay warm, but my body had other ideas. The blood that ran through my veins most have slowed to a leisurely pace. A nighttime stroll, with a loved one.

Link was here. Dani and Franny were too. I should have been excited, but I felt that something was wrong. Everything was wrong.

My blood ran cold.

Sam

Link was warm. He hugged me back as I held on to him. Maybe he wasn't mad. He was here. He came to find me. *Was it as simple as the fact that he liked me too?*

"We gotta' get somewhere warm. Liz probably has hypothermia." I knew how cold I was and she had been ambling around without a coat before she found me.

"What are you doing out here anyway," Franny asked.

"I don't really know. I just started walking and then I ended up here."

"Why didn't you just walk back?" Leave it to Franny to ask the obvious question.

"We tried. We just kept walking and walking and we never made it back to town."

122

"Um...it didn't take us that long to get here. It's only the bottom of the seventh." Franny held up her phone which had live notifications from the game.

"Children, we can argue later. Let's get Liz back to town." Link taking charge like that made my heart flutter. Then, my heart stopped.

Clank...Clank...Clank...Clank...

"What. Is. That?" Franny was obviously perturbed by the noise.

"I don't know but it's been creeping us out. We should leave." I was trying not to show it, but I was petrified. Link may have been too, but he definitely wasn't showing it. He held his phone up, shining light in every direction, seeking out the source of the noise. He illuminated nothing and then shut the light off before saying,

"Everyone turn off your flashlights." Franny and Dani killed the last two lights. "Notice anything?"

"Oh my God, where are the lights from the city?" Franny was most certainly panicking now.

Once again, we were trapped by the dark.

Franny

"Oh my God, where are the lights from the city?" No one said anything and if I couldn't feel Dani standing next to me, I would have thought I was alone. Link turned his light on again and I quickly followed suit.

"Okay, we know we came from that way," Link pointed behind me and Dani as he spoke. "Sam, you and I will help Liz and we'll just start walking that way."

"I don't think that will work. Liz and I tried that and we never saw any lights."

"We have to do something, Sam. We can't just si..."

Clank...Clank...Clank...Clank

Did that girlish shriek come from me? Why was I running?

I could hear voices shouting after me, but they were like background noise. I could hear footsteps behind me. I was being chased. I knew I had to run faster as the footsteps grew closer. My lungs burned. The voices grew faint, but the clanking kept getting louder and louder. The footsteps were on top of me and then I felt something cold and hard smash into the back of my head. I dropped my phone and it fell face up while I fell face down onto the tracks. My whole head felt warm and my eyelids were heavy. The voices were clear now.

"What did you do?" Sam's voice practically screeched.

"She needs a doctor!" Link was furious.

"Daddy?" Liz was sobbing.

I raised my head just enough to see my phone. The screen lit up with a notification,

> **Núñez homered to left (373 feet)**
> **Benintendi and Martinez scored.**

Then Sam shouted,

"No!" Then all was dark.

Link

Liz was heavier than she looked and it didn't help that Sam was freaking out and Liz was having a nervous breakdown. *Who was I kidding? I was freaking out and having a nervous breakdown.*

We were running as fast as we could with no direction other than to get away from what we just saw. Liz kept mumbling about her father and Sam just kept repeating "oh my God."

"Hold up!" My body needed a break and it was time to get some help. We laid Liz down gently and I dialed 911. I waited for the phone to ring, but when I pulled it away from my ear, I realized why it hadn't. "Shit!" Sam looked at me with worried eyes. I am sure mine looked worried to him as well as I uttered the words, "no service."

Liz

We were going to die. I knew that. Dani wasn't really Dani. She had the same black, hollow eyes as Daddy. I felt warm now. That was probably a bad thing.

"Stay away from us!" Link and Sam tried to drag me with them as Dani got closer.

"What's wrong with you?" Sam sounded bewildered.

"Can you bring me to Daddy," I asked. Dani grinned,

"Of course." She moved quicker than any human should be able to and shoved Sam and Link like they were paper dolls. With the light from Link's phone gone, all was dark. I felt Dani push me onto my back and I felt cold metal on my forehead.

Then, I felt nothing.

Sam

I knew something was wrong back at the bar. I should have just gone home. I got up slowly, listening, trying to find Link.

Clank.

"Link," I whispered as loudly as I could.

"Sammy," I heard whispered back. I stayed low to the ground but made my way towards the voice. "Sammy," it whispered again. It didn't sound like Link and I stopped dead in my tracks. "Sammy." The voice was right behind me.

"Sam!" Link's voice rang out from a least twenty yards away in front of me.

"Hiya, Sammy." Dani pushed me down and I felt the cold metal of the tracks on my hands as I tried to break my fall. Tears welled up in my eyes.

"Why are you doing this?" I tried to sound braver than I felt.

"You know. You can't make a deal with the Devil and not expect it to come due." I rolled over facing Dani's voice.

"A deal? What deal?"

"Are you kidding me?" Link found us. His flashlight showed Dani standing above me with a railroad spike in one hand. As he got closer, he continued, "you're killing us over a table at a bar?"

"A deal is a deal. Your prayers were answered, were they not?

"Bullshit!" Link was arguing with the Devil.

"Your friend warned you about messing with Devil."

"Well I know a thing or two about the Devil. Do deals really come due the same night they are made?" Link was bargaining with the Devil?

"Ugh," Dani became annoyed. "You people watch too much television." She lowered the spike. "So what, you want to renegotiate the terms, is that it?"

"Yeah. Yeah I do." Link sounded so sure of himself.

"Well, the Sox are winning so I am in a good mood. What are your terms?" Without hesitation Link replied,

"Sam goes free."

"Link, no!" He was offering up his life for mine.

"Sam, you don't deserve this." Link made his way over to me and stuck out his hand to pull me off the tracks. He turned to Dani, "Sam keeps his soul. Take mine." I couldn't let him do that. Dani raised her spike.

"Wait!" I wasn't going to let this happen.

"What," Dani asked. "I haven't agreed to his terms yet."

"Well I have better terms. You get both our souls, but after we both die our natural deaths. However we were going to die before all this

127

is how it shall be. Then, our souls are yours." Link looked at me as if he saw me for the first time. "What? I'm gay, I always just assumed that's where my soul was going anyway." A smile crossed his face.

"Let me get this straight," Dani broke up our moment. "You're both willing to sell your souls for love?" Without hesitation Link answered,

"Yes."

"And if your 'natural deaths' were supposed to be tomorrow?" *Could the Devil play Devil's advocate?*

"Then at least we'll have tonight," I said as I found Link's hand with mine. I didn't have to sound brave this time.

Link

I squeezed Sam's hand and looked the Devil straight in the eye.

"So, whaddya say? Deal?" Dani's phone buzzed and she dropped the spike to check it.

"It's your lucky night. The Red Sox won. Enjoy your lives, boys. See ya later." I blinked my eyes and Dani was gone.

"Thank God the Devil is a Sox fan, huh?"

"Not the time for humor, Link. Let's get outta' here."

At some point the city lights came back into sight and hand in hand we made our way back to where the night began. I was a completely different person than I was four hours ago, but a little soul-searching never hurt anyone.

128

Jael

I used the towel to wipe the mirror clear after I got out of the shower. The television was on in the living room. I didn't remember turning it on before I got in the shower. I smelled coffee brewing too. I wrapped the towel around me and ventured out to discover who was here.

The news anchor was talking about last night's game.

"The Red Sox took game one from the Dodgers last night with a final score of eight to four. The two teams face off in Boston again tonight with coverage starting at 7:30.
Coming up, a brutal double homicide shakes a New Hampshire town."

I clicked the tv off and went to the kitchen.

"I made coffee. Take it black?

"Like my soul." I took the mug from Dani's hand and kissed her on the cheek.

Acknowledgements

Thank you to Kerry White for helping to design the cover. Your artistic eye and fervent support of my work always help make me look better. LP4L.

To my friends, customers, and strangers who helped inspire the words between these covers, thank you. You may never know you were an inspiration, but the beauty of words will ensure your legacies last.

My absolute gratitude may never convey the necessary sentiments for Karen Baker. My boss, editor, friend, and family. Thanks for roping me into the "book biz" when I was 14 and believing there is something special about me. Your countless hours spent reading my work, even when you knew it would frighten you, can never be repaid.

To the cat who holds my heart, thank you for letting me write about your cute and crazy antics.

Last, but not least, this is all thanks to my mommy. After all, I wouldn't be here without her. You instilled in me the love of reading, writing, and cats. Who I am is a direct result of your accomplishments. Thank you for supporting me, loving me, and teaching me to live with no filter.

About the Author

Autumn Siders lives in New Hampshire with the world-famous cat, Emilita. She is the manager at The Country Bookseller where she has worked since she was 14. You can find more of her work on her blog, butwiththemind.com.

CPSIA information can be obtained
at www.ICGtesting.com
Printed in the USA
FFHW020708020119
50035408-54816FF